From the reviews of *Boobela and Worm*

'Joe Friedman's Worm is so gentle, funny and wise that it comes as no surprise to find that he unlocks Boobela's ability to heal others . . . There are not enough good books for this age range, and Friedman's sympathetic approach will make this one to re-read.'

Amanda Craig, *The Times*

'. . . a very sweet collection of stories set in a land of forbidden caves and haunting castles . . . an enchanting storybook for younger readers with charming illustrations by Sam Childs.'

Becky Stradwick, *The Bookseller*

'combines quirky originality with gentle simplicity in the text and in Sam Childs's images.'

Nicolette Jones, *The Sunday Times*

'Young children everywhere will delight in the adventures of Boobela and Worm.'

Publishing News

Boobela
and the
Belching
Giant

Acknowledgement

I'd like to thank Julia Giles for her help
with Worm's family tree J.F.

First published in Great Britain in 2007
by Orion Children's Books
a division of the Orion Publishing Group Ltd
Orion House
5 Upper St Martin's Lane
London WC2H 9EA
An Hachette Livre UK Company

1 3 5 7 9 10 8 6 4 2

Text copyright © Joe Friedman 2007
Illustrations copyright © Sam Childs 2007

Design by Sarah Hodder

The rights of Joe Friedman and Sam Childs to be identified as the author and illustrator of this work
respectively have been asserted.

All rights reserved. No part of this publication may be reproduced, stored in a retrieval system, or
transmitted, in any form or by any means, electronic, mechanical, photocopying, recording or
otherwise, without the prior permission of Orion Children's Books.

A catalogue record for this book is available from the British Library.

Printed in Great Britain

ISBN 978 1 84255 540 8

Boobela
and the
Belching
Giant

Joe Friedman
illustrated by Sam Childs

Orion
Children's Books

For Frederick,
Geant
good
wishes!
with love,
Joe Friedman

For Julie, who transformed my life
J.F.

For Ollie Burrows and Chester Isaacs, two
extraordinary boys, with love
S.C.

Worm looked at the map. Then he wriggled across the page and pointed. "What does belching mean?" he asked, puzzled.

"A belch is like a super-burp," explained Boobela. "Gas erupts from the bottom of your stomach and comes flying out of your mouth. It makes a really funny noise."

Worm wrinkled his nose. "You humans have some disgusting habits!"

"You can talk," Boobela laughed. "You eat mouldy vegetables, dried grass, and newspapers!"

Gran's
Island

Boobela's World

Mountain
City

Boobela's
Island

Smoky
Mountain

The Great
River

Titanic Falls

The Old Woods

Smelly
Swamp

Balloon
Launch
Field

Herne
Beach

Fjords

Boobela's
City

Pipeline
Surfing
Beach

Scarlet
Lake

Forbidden
Caves

Lake

Haunted Castle

Belching
Giant

Barton
Beach

Contents

Between each story, you can discover more about Boobela and Worm and the things they like to do.

Worm's Family Tree

The sky was filled with balloons. Big, beautiful hot air balloons. The Balloon Club was going on its Summer Outing to the cliffs of Barton Beach.

They had set out early to arrive at low tide. At high tide there would be no beach to land on!

They drifted over the flat landscape covered with small farms. Boobela could hear the voices of her friends calling to one another through the air.

Boobela had a thought. "Worm," she called.

Worm stuck his head out of his navigation box.

"If all worms are named Worm, how do you call to another worm?"

Worm looked embarrassed.

"I have a confession to make," he said. "I wasn't being entirely truthful when I said all worms are called Worm."

"You mean you have a proper name?" Boobela asked, stunned. She'd always known Worm as Worm.

Worm nodded.

"What is it?"

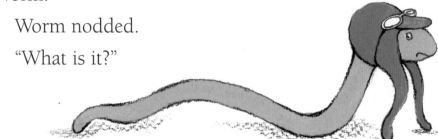

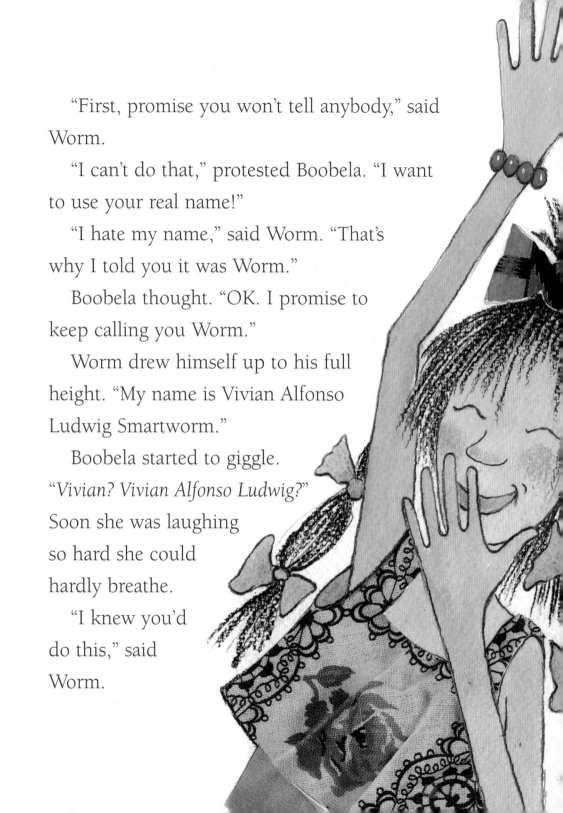

"First, promise you won't tell anybody," said Worm.

"I can't do that," protested Boobela. "I want to use your real name!"

"I hate my name," said Worm. "That's why I told you it was Worm."

Boobela thought. "OK. I promise to keep calling you Worm."

Worm drew himself up to his full height. "My name is Vivian Alfonso Ludwig Smartworm."

Boobela started to giggle. *"Vivian? Vivian Alfonso Ludwig?"* Soon she was laughing so hard she could hardly breathe.

"I knew you'd do this," said Worm.

"Just let me get
it out of my system,"
gasped Boobela. Her
laughter started to slow
down. "I never would have
guessed. Vivian!" And she
started off again. This time
she laughed so hard she almost
fell out of the wicker basket.

Worm just had to bear it. He
knew he had it coming. He
should have told her the truth
when she'd first asked.

Finally, Boobela was all laughed
out.

"Do all worms have family names that end with 'worm'?"

"Yes," said Worm. "There are the Fast and Slowworms, the Long and Shortworms, the Thin and Fatworms."

"Are you all friends?" asked Boobela.

Worm shook his head.

"Who don't the Smartworms get along with?" asked Boobela.

"The Longworms," said Worm.

"Why?"

"I don't really know," said Worm. "My parents told me we don't like them and never have."

"That's stupid," said Boobela. "You don't even *know* all the Longworms. How can you dislike someone you've never met?"

Worm shook his head. "It's just part of being a Smartworm."

"It doesn't sound very smart to me," said Boobela.

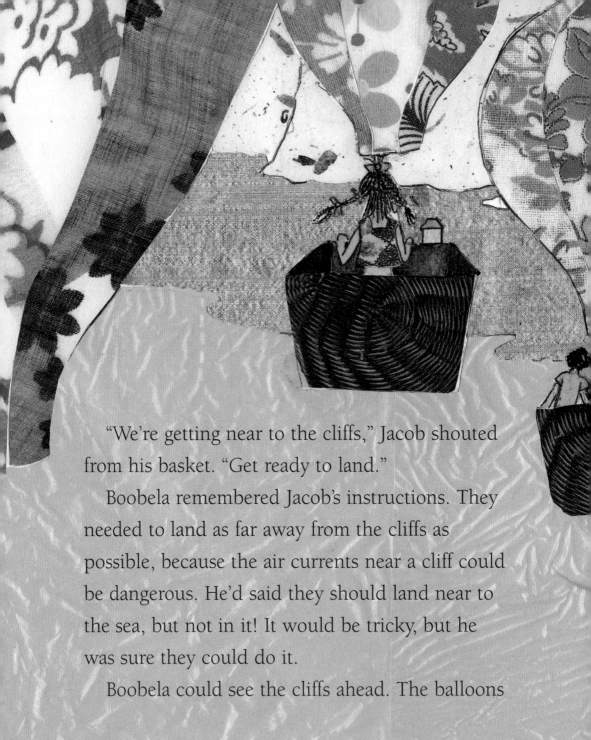

"We're getting near to the cliffs," Jacob shouted from his basket. "Get ready to land."

Boobela remembered Jacob's instructions. They needed to land as far away from the cliffs as possible, because the air currents near a cliff could be dangerous. He'd said they should land near to the sea, but not in it! It would be tricky, but he was sure they could do it.

Boobela could see the cliffs ahead. The balloons

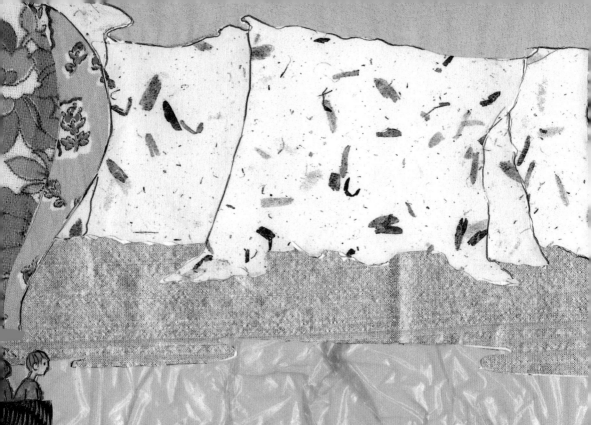

were starting to sink. She let out some air, then some more.

Immediately past the cliffs, she pulled hard on the parachute cord. There wasn't a lot of beach between the cliffs and the sea.

"Pull the rip cord!" Worm shouted.

Boobela did – and the balloon dropped like a stone. It bounced twice and landed on sand that was still wet from the tide.

"A bit bumpy, but right on target," shouted Jacob.

Everyone helped fold up the balloons. Then Jacob and Kate each formed a group, one to investigate the rock pools and one to look for fossils. Boobela couldn't decide which group to join – she wanted to do both!

She asked Worm. He couldn't decide either. In the end, Boobela flipped a coin. Kate's group won. Sophie wanted to carry Worm. As they walked towards a big tide pool, Kate said, "We might find crabs, small fish, barnacles, and maybe a few surprises."

Boobela and the children ran ahead of
Kate to be the first.

Nurgul shouted, "I've found a crab!"

She poked it
with a stick.

"That's a hairy crab," said Kate.

Sophie shouted, "Look, Worm! That shell is
moving!"

"I bet there's a hermit crab in there," said Kate.

She carefully picked up the shell and looked
inside. Then she showed it to Sophie and the other
children. Boobela leaned over to have a look.

"They're called hermit crabs because they live
in whatever sea shells they can find," said Kate.
"When they get too big for a shell, they have to
move to another one. Sometimes you can find one
between shells."

Worm was scanning the rock pool. He was
looking for relatives.

Kate continued, "If we find a couple of hermit crabs we could have a race. Look under the bits of seaweed."

Boobela and the children had a good search in the seaweed. There were several shouts as more crabs were discovered. They put them in the bucket that Kate had brought along.

"Uggh!" said Sophie when she turned over some seaweed. "What's *that*?"

Kate came over to look. "A candy-striped flatworm," she said.

"That's one of my cousins!" shouted Worm, excited.

"I don't think I'll be eating *that* piece of rock candy," said Sophie, wrinkling her nose.

Boobela, Kate and Nurgul laughed.

"You're much more handsome than that worm," whispered Sophie to Worm. Worm could see The Look in her eye. He ducked into his matchbox.

"Put me down. And no kissing!"

Sophie laughed and put Worm down near the flatworm.

"Have we got enough crabs for a race?" asked Tom, a red-haired boy who was new to the club.

They did.

"Ouch!" said Boobela, taking a crab from the bucket. "He nipped me! I'm going to call him Nipper!"

"Mine's called Speedy," said Tom. "Because I hope he wins."

Soon all crabs had names and the race began.

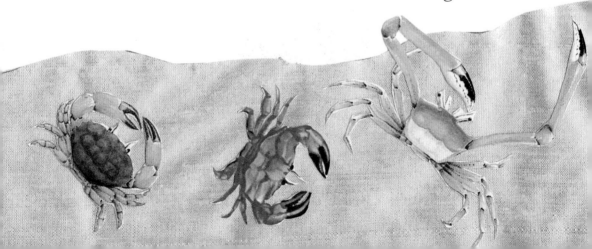

The children shouted and cheered.

Tom's crab came in first,
Sophie's second and Kate's third.
Nipper refused to move and
wouldn't start – however loudly
Boobela encouraged him.

Then they discovered a hermit crab without a
home. Tom picked it up carefully. Sophie and
Nurgul found some empty shells and put them
with the crab in a bucket. They watched in wonder
as the crab tried out each shell, easing himself into
each one backwards. Finally he found one that
suited him.

Jacob's group joined them. "We're hungry,"
said Jacob.

"Let's eat!"
shouted the
children.

Boobela helped Sophie, Tom
and Nurgul set out the picnic
lunch. It was a feast, with tons

of sandwiches and legs of chicken, three different
salads and four kinds of cakes – chocolate, lemon,
banana and a jam sponge.

"We've got less than two hours left till the tide
returns," Jacob called.

"I'd like to come with you this afternoon,"
Boobela said.

"Great," Jacob replied. They set off towards the
cliffs.

"Did you enjoy talking to the flatworm?" asked Boobela.

"He wasn't very interesting," said Worm, disappointed. "He'd never left the rock pool and all he could say was that this tide was really warm and that one was cold!"

Boobela laughed.

"It made me think how lucky I am to be travelling around on your shoulder!"

"That goes for both of us," said Boobela.

They arrived at the cliffs. Boobela knew from reading her mum's science books that the cliffs were made from layers of rock. The bottom layers were older than the top ones. There would be different fossils in each layer.

"How do you find a fossil?" asked Boobela.

"It's mostly a question of luck," said Jacob. "You break off a piece of chalk, clay or sandstone that looks interesting and slowly chip away at it."

The children showed Boobela the ones they'd discovered earlier. There were several sharks' teeth and many small, hard-shelled creatures.

"They're incredible!" exclaimed Boobela. "I hope *I* find something!"

Boobela could reach several layers higher than everyone else. She got on her tip-toes and pulled off a piece of loose sandstone. Worm peered at it as she broke it in half, then half once again. Nothing.

She repeated this again and again. Still nothing. It was very frustrating. It seemed all the other children were shouting excitedly with new finds.

"Only half an hour to go!" Jacob announced. Boobela knew she'd only be able to examine a few more pieces of sandstone.

"You found me deep under the ground at Gran's,"

said Worm. "You should be able to find a fossil in this cliff."

"I have magic inside me," Boobela reminded herself. She took several slow breaths and imagined finding a fossil.

She put her hands flat against the cliff wall and walked along. Suddenly her hands felt warm.

"Five minutes," shouted Jacob.

Boobela broke off a piece of sandstone. She looked at it carefully.

"See anything?" she asked Worm.

Worm shook his head. Boobela broke the piece in half.

"What's that?" asked Worm, pointing his head.

"It's a squiggle in the rock," said Boobela.

"It's not!" said Worm, excited. "It's a trail. A worm trail."

Boobela looked at the squiggle closely. It *did* look like a worm trail.

Jacob came over to see.

"What do you think that is?" asked Boobela.

"A worm trail," said Jacob, confidently.

"Were there worms that long ago?" asked Worm.

"People have found worm trails nearly five hundred million years old," said Jacob. He looked at his watch. "We've got to go! We've got six balloons to inflate!"

The children ran, calling to one another about what they'd found. Boobela took the worm rock with her.

"I want to show it to my mum and dad," Worm said. "I bet it's a Smartworm. My great-great-great-great-great grandfather!"

"You'll have to add a few more millions greats," said Boobela, laughing. "How do you know it's not a Longworm?"

"A Longworm?" Worm sniffed. "They wouldn't travel this far. They're all scared of their own shadows!"

"I have a funny feeling," said Boobela, "that someday you're going to meet a Longworm who is going to make you eat your words."

Worm laughed at the thought.

Worm's Sports Day

1. My favourite day is Sports Day. Worms come from miles around to the old wine cellar under the Johnsons' house.

2. There's a big space for lots of spectators and a floor made out of earth. It's like being outside without birds. Bliss.

5. Most worms hate water but for those who don't we have the One-metre Splash.

6. Everyone loves the Potato Push. It's hard to get them to go in a straight line.

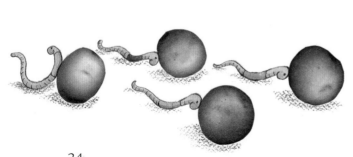

3. The first race is always the crawl. The half-metre crawl is like the hundred-metre dash. The winner is named the fastest worm.

4. Our marathon is the Ten-metre Crawl.

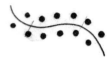

1. My favourite race is the One Metre Tunnel.

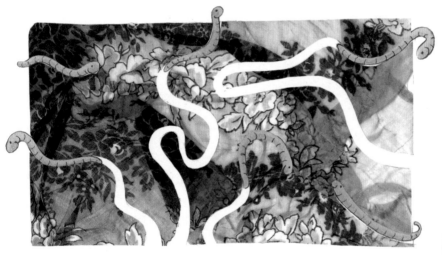

8. That's because I always win!

35

The Bet

Worm turned away. He couldn't bear to watch.
Boobela was eating dinner. To be exact: eight
frozen pizzas, six bags of crisps and four chocolate
bars. This wouldn't have been so bad if she hadn't
eaten eight frozen pizzas, six bags of crisps and
four chocolate bars *every* breakfast, lunch and
dinner *two weeks in a row*.

"What's wrong?" asked Boobela.

Worm nodded at her food.

"Why shouldn't I eat what I want?"

Worm crawled into his box to think. Boobela
would make herself sick eating like this. He was
Boobela's friend. He had to help her. But how?

• • •

The following day,
as Boobela explored her
garden, she noticed a
large, green metal
container. It was almost
hidden by vines.

"What's that?"

"A compost bin," said
Worm.

"What's a compost bin?"

"A restaurant for worms."

Boobela bent over and ripped
the vines off the top of the bin.
She lifted the lid and looked
inside. It was empty.

"The worms must be starving."

"They are," said Worm. "That
bin hasn't been filled since your
parents were here."

"When my mum cooked vegetables," said Boobela, remembering, "she'd always save the tops and bottoms of the carrots and beans, and all the cabbage and lettuce that had started to go rotten. Is this where she put them?"

Worm nodded. He was beginning to form a Plan.

"Yes, it was a great restaurant," he said.

"Worms eat all that rubbish?"

"It's not rubbish for worms. It's like pizza, hamburgers and ice cream for us."

Boobela giggled at the thought. Then she realised Worm was serious.

"What are the worms eating now?"

"There was no food here. They had to go elsewhere."

"That's awful," said Boobela. "I'll bring them some pizza crusts!"

"They wouldn't eat them," said Worm. "Worms eat things that grow."

"What *would* they eat, then?"

"The fruit and vegetables your mum gave them."

"But I don't like fruit or vegetables!"

Boobela didn't like thinking of Worm's family and friends as homeless. But she felt stubborn. She knew Worm was trying to get her to eat better . . . but she didn't want to!

Worm went on: "Did you know that we turn all the fruit and veg into good soil for the garden?"

Now Boobela *knew* Worm was pulling her leg.

"I don't believe you," she said. "Why don't I put some vegetables in the compost bin – and then give your worms a week to turn it into soil?"

"A week isn't enough," pleaded Worm. "It usually takes much longer."

"A week is all I'm giving you," said Boobela.

"OK," answered Worm. "Why don't we have a little bet to make it interesting?"

"You're on," Boobela responded. "If I win, you'll never complain about my eating again."

"And if I win," said Worm, "you'll have to eat enough fruit and vegetables to keep the compost bin full. For ever."

Boobela stopped to think. That was a pretty hefty penalty . . . but she couldn't lose. "OK," she replied.

Boobela repeated their bet as she shook Worm's tail.

"I'm not going to eat any of that rubbish now," Boobela declared. "I'm going off to get some old fruit and vegetables from my neighbours."

"Wait a second!" Worm protested, but it was too late. Boobela had already charged off.

Boobela returned from her trip with a large paper bag filled to the top. Worm told her how to fill the bin. When she was finished, Boobela inspected her handiwork.

"Yech!" she said, holding her nose. "It already smells. What's it going to be like in a week?"

"We'll see," said Worm.

• • •

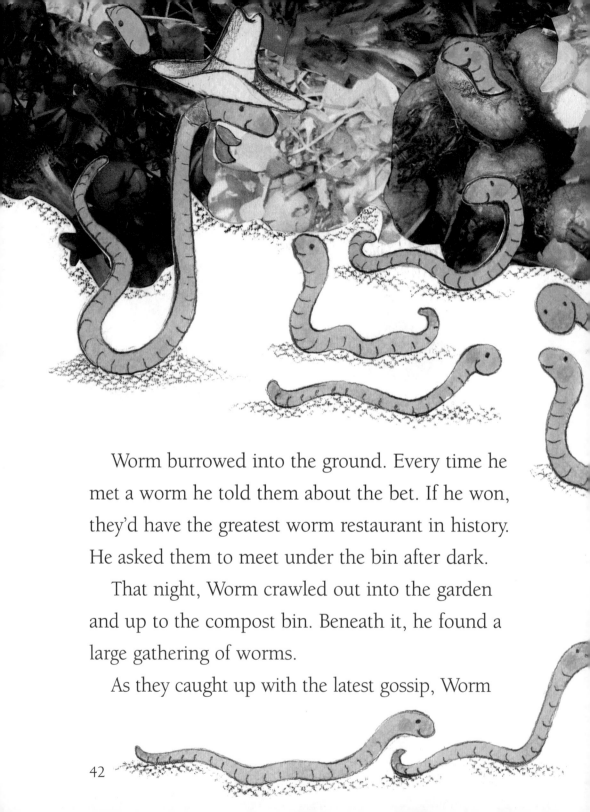

Worm burrowed into the ground. Every time he met a worm he told them about the bet. If he won, they'd have the greatest worm restaurant in history. He asked them to meet under the bin after dark.

That night, Worm crawled out into the garden and up to the compost bin. Beneath it, he found a large gathering of worms.

As they caught up with the latest gossip, Worm

 had to shout to be heard. "Listen up! This is important. If we can turn the stuff above us into soil in a week, we'll have food for ever."

Then he added, "And leave the top layer until the end. I want Boobela to think she's winning this bet."

The worms laughed. They all liked a good trick.

• • •

Every day, when she got up, Boobela went out to the compost bin to see how her bet was going. She could see that the vegetables she'd put on top hadn't moved.

Every night Worm crawled out to the garden to see how his family and friends were getting on. They were doing their best, but he could see they'd never finish on time. They needed help.

He crawled under the fence into the next garden. No compost bin. Then under the next fence. There was a big wooden one! He crawled underneath the bin and into the lovely warm stuff above. It was full of worms.

He called them together and told them about the bet.

After a silence, an old worm spoke up. "Impossible. You can't turn vegetables into compost in a week."

The worms started to crawl away.

"Wait a second," said an attractive young worm. "Granpa always thinks he knows everything. Just because it's never been done before doesn't mean we can't do it! Let's help Worm!"

"I agree," said someone else. "Besides, if there's always food in their compost bin, they won't be coming over here to eat ours! We should have a vote!"

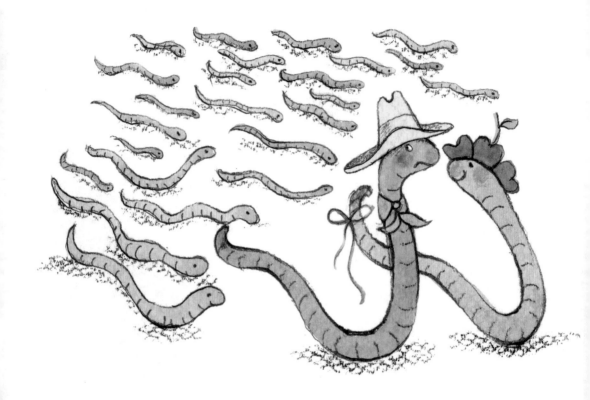

The "yes" side won. "Let's go and dig some compost!" shouted the young female worm. She and Worm led the way. Five hundred worms followed them.

The attractive worm said, "My name is Hannah Boadicea Longworm."

Worm's heart sank. She was a Longworm. If he told her his name, she wouldn't like him!

Then he had an idea.

"My name is Vivian Alfonso Ludwig . . . Worm."
he said, blurring the last word so that it couldn't be
understood.

Hannah hadn't caught his name. Worm breathed
a sigh of relief. They had a good chat as they
crawled toward the bin.

"I'll see you soon," he shouted. Hannah waved
and led the worms into the bin.

By the time Worm dragged himself back to
Boobela's house it was morning. He was exhausted.

Boobela woke up full of beans. She saw how
tired Worm was.

"You look terrible," she said. "Were you up all
night worrying? I don't want you to make yourself
ill, let's call off the bet."

Worm considered this. It still looked like he
would lose, but with worms from the other garden,
there might still be a chance.

"That's really kind of you," he said. "There's only two more days to go. I'll survive."

The next two days Boobela didn't bother checking the compost bin. And Worm was too tired to trek back to see how his fellow worms were doing.

So, as the sun rose on the seventh day, Worm felt glum. He didn't see how he could win . . . Still, he thought, it had been worth trying.

He insisted that Boobela have breakfast before she rushed up to check the compost bin, and he watched sadly as she ate four frozen pizzas, three bags of crisps and two chocolate bars. He had done his best – she would probably be eating the same meal until her parents got back or until she turned into a pizza herself, whichever came first.

"Ready?" Boobela asked.

"Let's do it," said Worm wearily.

Boobela bounced down the garden path to the compost bin. She lifted the lid. Worm closed his eyes. He didn't want to look. There was a long silence as Boobela stared inside.

"I don't believe it!" she exclaimed. She grabbed a garden fork and turned over the soil. It was *filled* with worms. Worm opened his eyes. He couldn't believe it either!

"They've done it!" both Boobela and Worm said at the same time.

Worm breathed a sigh

of relief, Boobela a sigh of dismay. She saw a horrible future in which she had to eat vegetables instead of pizza, potatoes instead of crisps, fruit instead of chocolate bars.

Worm did a perfect dive out of his box and into the bin. Then he burrowed into the soil.

"You did it!" he shouted. "You're all heroes!"

Hannah said proudly, "That'll show my granpa!" She imitated him saying "Impossible" and laughed.

Without thinking, Worm gave her a kiss. What had come over him? He'd kissed a girl! Hannah looked at him.

"Sorry," he said. "I'm just so happy!"

She smiled.

"It was very close. If you'd come at dawn we wouldn't have been ready. We'd better head back," Hannah said to her fellow worms. "I want everyone to look very low, as if we've failed. When my granpa starts to say I told you so, I'll tell him we did it!"

"She's just like me!" Worm thought.

He went up to the top of the heap and a very sad Boobela picked him up and put him in his box.

"We'd better go shopping," said Worm.

"And buy lots of fruit and vegetables . . ."

"I was getting sick of pizza, crisps and chocolate bars anyway," said Boobela. "I kept eating them because it made you so mad."

"There are lots of fruit and veg that taste great," Worm said.

Boobela looked doubtful. But a bet was a bet. They headed off to the greengrocer's.

"You can still eat a pizza now and then," said Worm.

Boobela brightened. "Thanks, pal."

2. You can also use an old garbage bin! Make lots of holes in the side because worms and compost need to breathe.

3. We worms like to eat all kinds of things: grass cuttings, shredded newspapers, uncooked vegetables and fruit, leaves, straw etc.

1. You'll need something to put your compost in. A simple container is four sticks of wood stuck in the ground with wire or plastic netting stapled around it. A plastic cover for the top.

4. What's important is to have a combination of wet things — vegetables and grass — and dry things — crunched up cardboard, paper, kitchen towels or newspaper. Half and half is the ideal. Try to mix wet with dry, especially if you use grass cuttings!

8. My relatives will find their way into the compost from the ground under it. Don't expect the compost to be finished in a week — you'll need every worm around for that!

7. Try to fill up the heap quickly. It won't start "cooking" until almost full.

6. Compost heaps don't like: meat, fish, fat, glossy magazines, weeds, thick roots, and processed food (pizzas!). These will also attract rats, so avoid!

5. If the compost gets too dry, add water. But not too much! Remember worms can drown and so can compost heaps!

The Fear Tree

"Look," said Worm, pointing his head towards a stand of twisted old trees not far from Gran's house. "Talk about spooky."

Boobela looked at the dark trees and shuddered. "Granpa mentioned them . . . They're called the Haunted Woods."

Gran had sent Boobela and Worm to buy some things at the shop at the far end of the island. This was the last thing Boobela wanted to do. She'd flown to Gran's because she wanted to have a magical adventure. But Gran was busy and she'd told Boobela she'd have to amuse herself. Boobela was not amused.

She walked along the muddy path to the shop.

"Do you think the woods are really haunted?" asked Worm.

"Granpa said he'd tried to walk through them at night. First he heard all kinds of strange noises. Then he saw two ghosts. He didn't stop to ask them questions. He just ran home."

"What kind of ghosts were they?" asked Worm, casually.

Boobela didn't answer. She was thinking about Gran being busy. She'd never been too busy before.

"Maybe Gran thinks I'm not ready to learn more magic. I'll have to prove to her that I am."

"How will you do that?" asked Worm.

Boobela was quiet again. "I don't know."

They were almost at the shop when Boobela noticed a tent in the garden of a large house.

"That's it!" she shouted, excited.

"That's what?" asked Worm.

"I'll show Gran I'm not a baby by camping in the Haunted Woods. Then she'll realise that I'm ready to learn more magic."

Worm frowned. "We've never camped before," he said. "If you want to sleep in a tent, we could do it in Gran's garden."

"What would that prove?" said Boobela. "I want to show her I'm not scared of anything."

"But maybe you should be scared of some things," said Worm. "Like ghosts." Worm wasn't scared of many things. Birds and water, as Boobela knew. And ghosts, as she didn't.

Boobela hesitated. She was a little frightened of ghosts herself.

"I'm a giant," she said, trying to convince herself. "And I have magic in me . . . Ghosts won't want to bother me . . ."

"But what if they do?" Worm persisted. He really didn't want to sleep in those woods.

"I never knew you were such a scaredy worm," said Boobela. "Stop worrying. It'll be an adventure!"

• • •

"Are you *sure* you want to camp there?" asked Gran later that day.

"Of course," said Boobela, trying to hide her doubts. "It'll be fun!"

"All right," said Gran. "Here's our tent. The instructions are inside the canvas bag. It wasn't designed for a giant, so it might be a bit cramped."

Boobela found a clearing in the Haunted Woods.

Worm watched as she chose a piece of flat ground and laid out the tent. She hammered in the pegs and put the poles up. Finally, she tied the ropes to the sides and pegged them down.

The tent was up! She felt pleased. She looked around. The sun was beginning to set and birds were chattering away in the trees.

"This won't be so hard," she said to herself.

They returned to Gran's house. Gran
needed help preparing dinner so Boobela went out
to the garden to pick vegetables. She carefully
scraped off the soil and put it in a separate dish for
Worm. Then she cut up the vegetables. Gran made
them into a lovely stew.

At dinner, Granpa said, "Nothing like freshly
picked vegetables."

"Or freshly scraped soil," added Worm.

They all laughed.

After dinner Boobela brushed her teeth. Gran lit
an oil lantern and gave it to her. "Have a good
time," she said.

Boobela held the lantern as they walked through the woods. It cast huge, moving shadows on the crooked old trees. Boobela was sure she could see a couple of large animals following them, just behind the trees. Were there wolves on Gran's island?

She tried to whistle, to show that she wasn't scared. But her mouth was so dry the whistle just didn't seem to want to come out.

As they walked further into the woods, Boobela heard an animal howl.

"That doesn't sound very big . . ." said Boobela. She wanted Worm to reassure her.

"It sounded pretty big – and hungry – to me," declared Worm.

This was not what Boobela wanted to hear. Even though she was probably bigger than any animal in the woods she was still a child. And she didn't have sharp teeth . . .

Boobela breathed a sigh of relief when they got to the clearing.

She put the lantern in the tent and sat with Worm outside. Their eyes got used to the dark.

"Look," said Boobela, pointing to the stars. "There are thousands of them."

"Millions! Zillions!" said Worm. Worm hadn't really seen stars before.

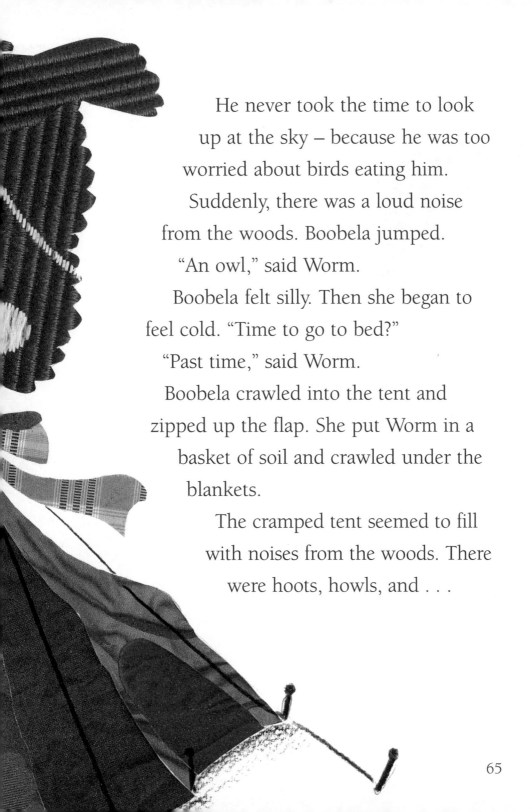

He never took the time to look
up at the sky – because he was too
worried about birds eating him.

Suddenly, there was a loud noise
from the woods. Boobela jumped.

"An owl," said Worm.

Boobela felt silly. Then she began to
feel cold. "Time to go to bed?"

"Past time," said Worm.

Boobela crawled into the tent and
zipped up the flap. She put Worm in a
basket of soil and crawled under the
blankets.

The cramped tent seemed to fill
with noises from the woods. There
were hoots, howls, and . . .

echoey hiccups. Boobela wasn't too troubled about the hoots and howls. They were made by smaller animals. It was the hiccups that worried her. What could hiccup like that? She shuddered as she thought, *Ghosts . . .*

"I don't think I'll ever go to sleep," she said.

Worm hiccupped again. Normally he would have said "Excuse me," but he felt embarrassed. He knew he'd eaten his dinner too quickly.

Boobela didn't realise that it was Worm who had hiccupped. *That ghost is very close*, she thought nervously.

After a while the hiccups stopped, and eventually Boobela fell asleep. Then she had a dream . . .

She was walking along a dark tree-lined street.
Worm wasn't with her. His box wasn't even on
her shoulder. She felt very alone. And scared.
Like something horrible was about to happen.
Just as she thought this, three huge ghosts came
from behind a house and started flying towards
her. Boobela screamed. She turned and ran. The
ghosts chased her. They came closer and closer.

"Boobela! Boobela! Are you OK?"

Boobela woke.

"I think you were having a nightmare," said Worm.

Boobela sat up and bumped her head against the top of the tent. She remembered where she was. Then she told Worm her dream. "It seemed so real," said Boobela.

"Why don't you tell Gran?" suggested Worm. "I bet she knows about dreams."

"Well done," said Gran, when Boobela and Worm arrived at the barn in the morning.

Boobela was almost too tired to reply. She hadn't been able to go back to sleep after her nightmare, because she was frightened the ghosts would come in another dream.

She told Gran over breakfast. "I was thinking about ghosts before we went to sleep," she added. "Do you think that might have made me dream about them?"

"Some people would say that," Gran replied. "I'd say you had this dream to show that you can change what happens in your dreams."

"You mean I could have got rid of the ghosts?" asked Boobela.

"You could, but it's easier to change how you feel. You were scared because you were all alone."

Boobela was surprised. "You mean . . . I didn't have to be on my own?"

"Of course not," said Gran. "You have the power to call anyone you want in a dream – Granpa or me, your mum or dad, Worm or your friends at the Balloon Club . . . or all of us . . ."

Boobela felt all fired up. "You mean all I have to do is call someone and they'll come?"

Gran nodded.

"How will that help?" asked Worm.

"You won't be so frightened if you're not on your own. That will make whatever is scaring you less powerful. *And* your friends can bring you something to help."

"Like what?" Boobela wanted to know.

"A mirror," said Gran. "Ghosts are scared of mirrors."

Boobela was so excited she wanted to go right back to sleep. But she knew ghosts only come at night and Gran had other plans. She wanted Boobela to help her build a sheltered veranda for Granpa.

Boobela was so busy that it seemed no time until it was dark. The floor of the deck was finished and she'd started on the roof.

Granpa told her how much he was looking forward to sitting on the new veranda.

After dinner, Gran said, "Before you go to sleep, I'll going to teach you something that will help you whenever you're frightened."

"Not just in dreams?" asked Worm.

"If you're scared of having bad dreams, you can do it before you go to sleep. But it will help any time you're scared."

Gran walked with Boobela and Worm to their tent. Inside, Boobela snuggled down into the blankets.

"Close your eyes," said Gran.

"Can I do it too?" asked Worm.

"Of course," said Gran. "Imagine you're in a magic garden." She waited a minute. "Are you there?"

"Yes," said Boobela. "The colours are amazing."

"Ummm," said Worm. "The soil is lovely."

"Now, in the garden there is a very special tree: The Fear Tree. It's big and strong. Can you find it? Worm, you'll have to find the roots."

"I've found it," said Boobela.

"Me too," said Worm.

"Good," said Gran. "Now, hang all your fears and worries up on the tree. They may be different colours and shapes. Tell me when you're done."

Boobela imagined
her fear of ghosts as a big
brown shadow. She hung it
up on a large branch of the
tree. "I've done it," she said.

Worm imagined his fear as a
black bird with a large beak.
He attached it to the roots of
the tree. "Me too," he said in a
sleepy voice.

"Now," said
Gran, "just play in
the garden until you fall asleep. The Fear Tree
will hold all your fears and worries until the
morning. You might even find they've disappeared
. . . Sweet dreams!"

Boobela was having so much fun playing in her
magic garden she didn't notice any noises from the
woods, or Gran leaving. Soon she was fast asleep.

In the morning, Boobela awoke with a huge grin. She jumped up, grabbed Worm's basket, and ran back to the barn.

"It worked!" she shouted, excitedly as soon as she saw Gran.

"What happened?" said Gran and Worm together.

"The ghosts came again," said Boobela. "I was scared but I remembered what you'd said. I have magic in me, I thought. I decided to call Worm to help."

"Me?" asked Worm, very pleased.

"Who else?" said Boobela. "You came, but you were huge. Much bigger than me. And you were holding a giant mirror in your mouth!"

Worm laughed with delight. He'd always wanted to be big!

"As soon as the ghosts saw you and the mirror they started getting smaller. I said 'Boo!' and they turned and flew away, as fast as they could.

We both laughed and I gave you
a big hug."

"Well done," Gran said, "You
can always tell who your true
friends are – they're the ones
who help in your dreams."

Worm and Boobela looked at
each other. They smiled.

Letters from Mum and Dad

The letter was sealed with red wax. Boobela's heart leaped. It was from Mum and Dad! But it was early. Was something wrong?

She tore the letter open. Worm looked down from her shoulder as she read it aloud.

Oh no!

Dear Boobela,

We were very upset to hear that Granpa is still ill and that Gran hasn't returned to take care of you.
We're going to have to cut our expedition short so you're not home alone.

It is a shame. We've finally found someone who can lead us to a famous wise man we've been trying to find. He'll be able to tell us all about the local healing plants.

We're pleased to hear about Worm. Tell us more about him.

I know what I'll do. I'll tell them you got me to eat vegetables and keep tidy and wash my toes. And that I'm reading lots of books and having lots of fun. Then they'll realize I'm fine and there's no rush to get back."

We miss you very much
and wish we could come
home every night to give
you a hug and a kiss but
sadly that's not possible.

All our love,
Mum and Dad.

It's not that I don't love
them, Worm. I do. Or
that I don't miss them.
I do. But it's just that for
the first time I'm feeling brave
and able to explore the world.
If they come home now we
couldn't have so many
adventures.

Worm nodded. He could have his mother
and father *and* adventures too. She had to
make a choice.

They'll be home soon enough,
and maybe you'll have had your
fill of adventures by then ...

Boobela smiled. She would
definitely tell her parents how lovely it was
to have a friend who really understood what
she was feeling. Just like they did.

Boobela and the Belching Giant

Boobela's hands were sticky
with goo as she put the
finishing touches on her
volcano. She'd made it out of salt,
vegetable oil, and flour. In the
middle was a bottle filled almost to
the top with water, red food
colouring, washing up liquid and
baking soda. Without thinking,
she wiped her hands on her apron.

"Worm! Wake up," she shouted.
"The eruption is about to begin."

A tired-looking Worm emerged from his box.

"This had better be good," he grumped.
"What happened to your apron?"

Boobela showed
Worm her hands. They
were still gooey.
"Yuck," he said.
Boobela ignored him and
opened a bottle of vinegar.
"Ready?" she asked, eager to get
started. The sharp smell of vinegar
filled the room. Boobela's nose wrinkled.
"As I'll ever be," said Worm.
Boobela poured the vinegar into the
water bottle. It started to bubble. Thick
red liquid rose up and flowed down the
sides of the volcano.
"Cool!" said Boobela.
"Moderately impressive," said
Worm. "Why don't we go
and see the real thing?"

• • •

Boobela's balloon drifted high over the stony ground.

"It should be just beyond the next hill," shouted Worm. "Open up. I want to see it!"

Boobela took the cover off Worm's navigation box and lifted him up to her shoulder. As they passed over the hill, the giant volcano came into view.

"It's not as big as I expected," said a disappointed Worm.

"That's because we're so high above it, you daft worm," said Boobela.

They looked down. The balloon passed over the volcano. Deep inside it, they could see lava glowing red. A bubble formed in it and then burst. The volcano had belched!

A cloud of hot gases
rose towards the
balloon and pushed it up
towards the clouds.

"Stinkarooney!" said Boobela. "That smells like
a million rotting eggs!"

"Lovely," said Worm, taking a deep breath.

• • •

Boobela put on her rucksack, filled with water and treats. She helped Worm into his matchbox on her shoulder and they headed up the volcano.

As they got closer to the top there were fewer and fewer plants. The ground was hard and uneven, as if an enormous hand had raked its fingers across it. Boobela was glad she was wearing her walking boots. The rocks were so jagged they would have torn up her trainers.

It was hard work climbing, even for a giant. Boobela stopped to drink some water and eat a very large sandwich. Worm was too excited to eat. The smell of the volcano got stronger the higher they went.

It took several hours for Boobela to reach the top. As they got near, they ran into a party of children.

Boobela
didn't feel
worried as
she approached
the oldest. "My
name is Boobela and
this is my friend Worm."
He replied, "My name is
Rob. I haven't seen you here before."
"It's my first time," replied
Boobela. "And last, if I have any
choice." She pointed to her nose.
"You get used to it," said Rob.
"You're well prepared," said
Boobela, pointing to Rob's shoes.
"I've been up eight times already. I
kept having to buy new shoes, so I
found these studs. I just clip them on
to whatever shoes I'm wearing!"

Rob's group surrounded Boobela, glad for a chance to take a break from climbing.

A small boy spoke to Worm. "This is my first time too!" he said enthusiastically. Then he remembered his manners. "My name is Joey."

"Pleased to meet you," said Worm. "Don't mind her. She likes to complain."

"We're a volcano club," explained Joey. "We've read all about the Belching Giant and now we're here! It's bigger than I thought! And it smells like my granpa's feet!"

Worm remembered the first time he met Boobela. 'Your feet stink,' he'd said. He laughed.

"We'd better get going," said Rob. "Otherwise we won't get to the top and down again before dark."

"It can't be far now," said Boobela.

"If you're tired, think about them," said Rob, pointing to Joey and the other smaller children. "They've got much shorter legs."

Boobela grinned. "I can carry someone on my shoulders!"

A raft of hands went up. Boobela closed her eyes, spun in a couple of circles and then pointed. Her fingers were almost touching Joey! He shouted with glee.

"I'll take someone else on the way down," said Boobela to the others.

Boobela bent down and Joey climbed up.

"This is great," he said. "I can see for miles! And I can talk to Worm."

"Tell me more about your granpa's feet," said Worm.

While Worm and Joey chatted, Boobela asked Rob, "Why do you climb up here so often?"

"I collect plants," replied Rob. "Ones that grow on volcanoes. Today I'm hoping to find a rare plant that only flowers this time of year."

"My parents collect plants too!" Boobela said. "They're botanists. They've been away in the Dabushta Jungle for months. They're looking for plants that heal people."

Soon they reached the top.

Boobela and the others looked over the edge into the volcano.

Worm was thrilled. "Just imagine," he said. "If I kept tunnelling down in the garden I'd end up in the centre of the earth."

"You'd be a roasted worm," said Joey.

Worm nodded. "It's probably not such a good idea."

Rob took a pair of binoculars out of a pocket in his rucksack. He scanned the walls of the volcano with them.

"Look," he said, pointing. "There's a flower!"

Boobela craned her neck to see. "I can see it!" she said. "But it's too far down to reach!"

"Maybe not," said Rob with a grin.

He removed some long lengths of metal from his rucksack and started to fit them together.

Meanwhile, Joey played with Rob's binoculars.

He pointed them at Worm. He looked huge!

Boobela looked through them and laughed. Then Joey turned the binoculars the wrong way around and aimed them at Boobela. She was the size of an ordinary girl! He showed Worm.

"Sometimes Boobela wishes she was this size," said Worm.

When Rob was finished, he had a long pole with a basket and claw at the far end.

"That's really clever!" exclaimed Boobela.

"I invented it myself," replied Rob proudly.

Rob extended the pole towards the flowers. The basket and claw weren't nearly long enough.

"I'll have a go," volunteered Boobela. "Grab my feet."

Rob held onto Boobela's feet and Joey and the others held onto Rob. Boobela lay down and, little by little, wriggled off the edge.

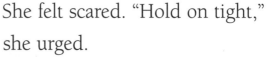

She looked below her. It was a long way down.

She felt scared. "Hold on tight," she urged.

"We will!" Rob and the children chorused.

Boobela held out the pole as far as she could – but the flower was still an arm's length away.

She looked down. Below her was a small rock ledge. She could easily get the flower from there.

"Pull me back," she said.

She pointed to the ledge. "I'm going to jump down there."

"I don't think that's a good idea,"
Rob said. "I'm not sure it could take
your weight. And anyway, how would you
get back up?"

"You could pull me," Boobela replied. "Using my
belt."

"It's too risky," said Rob.

Boobela felt stubborn. She knew this would
work. And she wanted to get that flower for her
new friend. She took a deep breath and leaped
down to the ledge.

"Hand me the pole," she said.

Rob did. Boobela stretched and carefully used Rob's invention to remove the flower and the tiny bit of earth it was growing in. She held the pole out to Rob above her.

He removed the flower.

"Stand close to where the ledge is thickest," urged Rob. "Tie your belt on. Then I'll pull it up."

Boobela began to untie her belt. Suddenly, there was a loud crack! A chunk of the ledge she was standing on broke off and disappeared into the volcano.

"Don't move!" shouted Rob.

The ledge shuddered. There was horrible deep rumbling noise and another bit of the ledge cracked and fell. Boobela hugged the side of the volcano. THUMP! The ledge beneath her exploded. Boobela tumbled into the volcano.

"Boobela! Worm!" the children above her screamed.

Boobela landed on another ledge. She scrambled
to where the ledge was strongest. She looked up.
Even if she could stand on her own head she
couldn't reach the others.

Boobela panicked. She was so frightened she
couldn't think. She could hardly breathe. Worm

stuck his head out of his matchbox. He looked up where the children were screaming. Then he saw Boobela's white face.

"Breathe," he whispered.

Boobela took a deep breath, then another. Some colour returned to her face. "Worm," she cried, "I've made a really big mistake! We can't get back!"

"You're scared," said Worm. "Remember what Gran said about being scared."

Boobela thought of her Gran's smiling face. That helped her calm down a bit. She remembered what her Gran had said to do when she was scared. She closed her eyes and started to count her breaths. One, two, three . . .

Then she went to her imaginary garden. She could see it clearly in her mind. She stood in front of her Fear Tree. She took off her fear – it was like a big black overcoat – and hung it up in the tree. Immediately, she felt better. She opened her eyes.

Rob had managed to calm the children down.

"Thanks," said Boobela.

Worm looked at her closely. "Good to have you back."

The volcano belched. Boobela held her nose. Then she started to laugh.

"As if we don't have enough trouble," she giggled. "Now, the Belching Giant is trying to stink us to death."

Worm laughed too. "Let's figure out how to get out of this mess."

Boobela looked up. It was definitely too far for the volcano club to pull her, even if they had a rope, which they didn't. She had to think of something else. She looked closely at the wall of the volcano. It was pitted with holes, where lava bubbles had burst thousands of years earlier.

She pointed out the bubbles to Worm. "Do you think I could climb?"

Worm looked at Boobela's boots. "They won't grip."

Boobela nodded and thought. She couldn't borrow anybody else's shoes – her feet were too big.

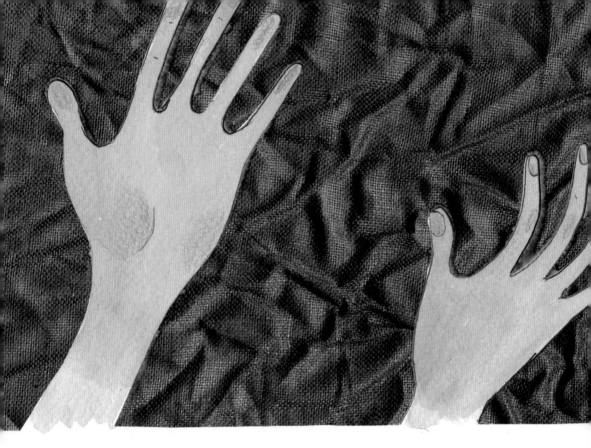

Then she had an idea.

"Rob," she yelled. "Throw down your studs."

"I don't think they're big enough," yelled Rob.

"Don't worry," said Boobela. "I know what to do."

Rob took off his studs. He looked down at Boobela.

"I'm not good at throwing," he said. "What if I miss?"

"Get Joey to do it," said Worm. "He plays
cricket. He's a wicket keeper!"

Joey stepped forward. He looked down at Boobela.

"No problem," he said. He took the studs from
Rob. "Ready?" he shouted to Boobela.

She nodded.

Joey threw the studs directly into Boobela's
hands, one at a time.

"Good throws!" shouted Worm. Joey felt pleased and proud.

Boobela took off her belt. She took out a knife from her rucksack, then cut the belt in two. Using one half of it, she tied a set of studs onto the front of her left boot. Then she used the other half to tie the second set onto her right boot.

"Get everybody back," she shouted to Rob. "I don't want a lot of noise as I climb."

Rob took the children away. Boobela looked at Worm.

Worm put on his best cowboy accent. "Let's get out of here, pardner."

Boobela smiled. She grabbed one of the holes in the wall high above her,

then found a place for her feet.
She tested the studs. They were on
firmly. She started to climb the wall. She
tried out each handhold and foothold before
she put her weight on it. She didn't want to
repeat her mistake.

It was hard work. Her hands got cut on
the rocks. But Boobela was very
determined. She didn't want to let Worm
down. Metre by metre she rose.

Then she felt someone grab her hands.
It was Rob. She'd reached the top! Rob
helped her over the edge. Shouting with
relief, the volcano club climbed all over
her.

The volcano belched again.

"I think it's disappointed it didn't have
me for dinner," said Boobela. She
looked at Rob.

"That's the last time I jump into a volcano. I hope it was worth it."

"It was." Rob smiled. "We're the first to discover these flowers! Did you know that the person who finds a new plant gets to name it?" Rob added.

"Really?" said Boobela. "What will you call it?"

"I think I'll call it *Boobelosa Fantastico*."

The children cheered.

"Wow," said Worm. "Your mum and dad will be really proud!"

Boobela smiled. As soon as she got home, she'd write to them about it. She couldn't wait.

How I Came to Write
the Boobela and Worm Stories

One night at bedtime, my daughter demanded I make up a story. Right away! I cast desperately around for an idea. "How about a story about something big and something small?" I thought. A moment later I had a girl giant, Boobela. I imagined her in the garden. What would be *small* there? A worm! And what would he say to her . . .

When growing up, I felt different from other children because my parents were deaf. They felt different too. This experience helped me write about Boobela. When I was older, I did research exploring the hidden abilities of the mind. I learned everyone has special magic in them.

I live in London with my wife and daughter. We also have a Bengal cat and a golden retriever dog. When I'm not writing, I work as a psychotherapist. I help people solve problems and enjoy themselves. Boobela is learning to do this. I hope you do too!

Joe Friedman

Visit Joe Friedman's website at www.boobela.com

. . . and time to meet Sam Childs

Sam Childs is the precocious offspring of Susie Jenkin-Pearce. Even before the age of one, Sam was painting pretty presentable zebras. Leaving home brought about a change in style, and Sam now creates luscious fabric designs using a vast collection of theatre costumes.

*Have you read Boobela and Worm's
first book of adventures?*

Boobela
and
Worm

Boobela is a young giant – shy and lonely because everyone runs away from her. Worm is mischievous and courageous, clever and wise. When they meet, Boobela's world changes. She learns to be brave and discovers magic. Together they fly hot-air balloons, play games on the beach – and make lots of new friends.